Foxes

Written by
Jill Atkins

Ransom

What do foxes look like?

A fox has:
- ✓ a tan coat with white on its chest
- ✓ sharp, pointed ears
- ✓ a pointed nose
- ✓ a long bushy tail called a brush

Foxes are wild animals.
They are mammals, like us.

They can smell, hear
and see very well.

The male fox is sometimes
called a **dog fox**.

The female fox is called
a **vixen**.

Foxes make their homes in all sorts of places. It might be:
- ✓ under tree roots
- ✓ in a hole under the ground
- ✓ under a shed

Their home is called a **den**.

Little foxes sitting outside their den

In spring, the vixen has her **cubs** inside the den.

There are between four and six cubs in the litter.

The cubs are helpless when they are born.
They cannot see or hear.
They have no teeth.

The vixen feeds her cubs on milk.

After a few weeks, the cubs
can come out of the den.
They are very playful.

The dog fox and the vixen hunt.

Foxes are **predators**. This means they hunt and kill animals for food.

When the cubs are little, the dog fox finds food for himself and the vixen.

This is because the vixen needs to stay to look after the cubs.

What do foxes eat?
They eat many things!
They eat:
- ✓ rabbits
- ✓ birds
- ✓ insects
- ✓ other small animals

Foxes sometimes find food on rubbish tips or in dustbins!